KITTEN KINGDOM

∽ Tabby and the Catfish ∽

Tabby and the Catfish

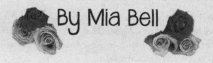

By Mia Bell

Scholastic Inc.

With special thanks to Conrad Mason

For Emma McGeachie

All rights reserved. Published by Scholastic Inc., *Publishers since 1920*, 557 Broadway, New York, NY 10012, by arrangement with Working Partners Limited. Series created by Working Partners Limited, London. SCHOLASTIC and associated logos are trademarks and/or registered trademarks of Scholastic Inc. KITTEN KINGDOM is a trademark of Working Partners Limited.

ISBN 978-1-338-29236-7

10 9 8 7 6 5 4 3 2 1   19 20 21 22 23

Printed in the U.S.A.   40
First printing 2019
Book design by Baily Crawford

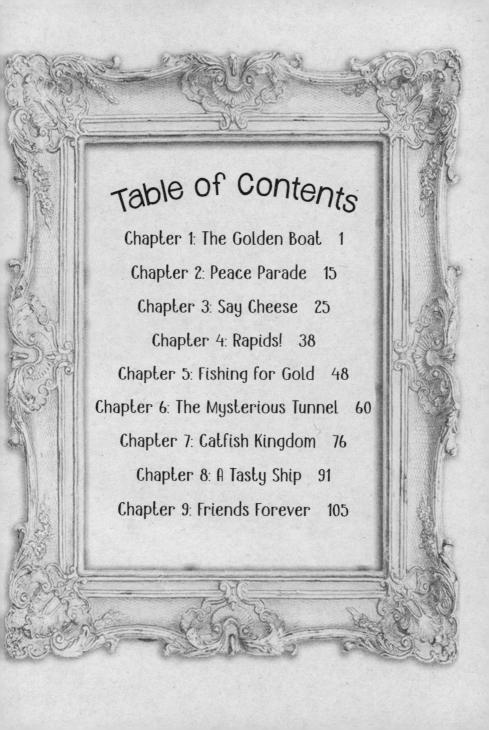

Table of Contents

Chapter 1

THE GOLDEN BOAT

"Raise the anchor!" cried Princess Tabby.

"Set sail!" said her younger brother, Leo.

"Stop rushing me!" grumbled Felix, their older brother.

The royal kittens were crouching on a grassy bank in the palace gardens. The river ran past, crystal clear and sparkling in the sunshine. *It's the perfect day to try out our toy boat*, thought Tabby. *If only Felix would stop messing with it!* The black cat was carefully checking every sail to make sure they were on straight.

"Let me do it!" said Leo, reaching for the boat. But Felix pulled it away and set it gently in the water.

"Wow!" they all gasped together. The boat sailed along, ticking like a watch. Their friend Clawdia's father had made it out of shining gold. It had a little clockwork engine, moving sails, and an anchor that went up and down.

"It's the best toy ever," said Tabby as the boat sailed under a stone bridge.

"I'll get it on the other side," called Leo. He ran off in a flash of orange fur.

"But it's my turn next!" yelled Tabby. She chased after him.

"Careful!" shouted Felix, following. "Don't break it!"

The three kittens ran along the riverbank, their tails waving behind them. Tabby was the first one past the bridge, and the first to see the boat come bobbing out. *There it is!* Tabby leaned over the water, reaching as far as she could . . .

"Whoops!" cried Felix.

Tabby turned and saw him slip on the wet grass. He grabbed Leo's paw, but Leo wobbled and bumped into Tabby. *Thump!* Tabby lost her balance. She waved her paws and stuck out her tail. But it was no good.

SPLASH!

All three royal kittens plunged into the river.

The cold water soaked Tabby. She splashed and shivered. "It's horrible!" she cried. She hated getting wet, just as much as any other kitizen in Mewtopia.

"My whiskers are stuck to my face!" wailed Felix, popping up next to Tabby.

"I'VE GOT WATER IN MY EARS!" yelled Leo. "I CAN'T HEAR A THING!"

Tabby tried to stay calm. *A kitty hero shouldn't be afraid of a little water . . .* "Let's kitty-paddle back to the bank," she said. "Like Nanny Mittens taught us."

Together, the royal kittens kicked hard with their back paws and paddled with their front paws. They splashed their way back to the grass and pulled themselves up. They sat, panting on the bank. Their fur was all flat, and water dripped from their whiskers.

"Leaping fleas!" said Felix. "I'm glad that's over."

"Did anyone get the boat?" asked Leo, rubbing his ears.

Tabby spotted it drifting away from them. "There it is!" She pointed. But it was already out of reach, and moving fast in the current.

"We'll never get it back now," said Leo sadly. "It was my favorite toy."

"It's not *yours*," said Felix. "And it wouldn't even have floated if I hadn't fixed the sails."

"But if *you* hadn't been so clumsy, we never would have lost it!" said Tabby.

"That's enough!" said a familiar meow.

The royal kittens turned. King Pouncalot and Queen Elizapet were walking over the grass toward them, dressed in their crowns and red capes. Normally Tabby was glad to see her parents. But today they looked very annoyed.

King Pouncalot gave each kitten a stern look. "Haven't we warned you about playing near water? We're cats, for meow's sake!"

"And all this arguing," added Queen Elizapet. "Today of all days!"

"The Peace Parade will begin soon," said King Pouncalot. "And here you are, fighting . . . Well, I'm afraid we can't let you ride on the royal boat with us now."

The royal kittens gasped.

"But we always go on the royal boat!" cried Tabby.

"We *love* the Peace Parade," added Felix. "All the different boats, and the kitizens cheering, and the brass band playing . . ."

"You'll have to watch all that from beside the river," said Queen Elizapet.

"But—" began Leo.

"Not another word," said Queen Elizapet. "Back to your room to get dry!"

Tabby and her brothers were still shivering and dripping as they went through a side door into the palace courtyard. Tabby felt ashamed. *I can't believe we ruined our chance to be part of the Peace Parade!*

"What's going on over there?" said Felix.

Tabby saw a little crowd of cat lords and

ladies by a door, talking excitedly. They all wore their best clothes, ready for the Peace Parade.

"Make way!" called a voice from inside. Then Captain Edmund came marching out. The big orange tomcat was wearing his shiniest silver armor, and in one paw he held a golden torch. Magical orange flames flickered from the end.

"Meowza!" gasped Leo. "It's the Torch of Peace!"

Tabby couldn't help it—her tail flicked with excitement. "Last one there's a stinky rat!" she called.

"Mom and Dad said..." began Felix. But Tabby was already running across the courtyard, leaving wet paw prints behind her. She pushed through the crowd, with Leo, then Felix, following.

"Slow down there, kitties!" cried Captain Edmund. He held the torch away from them. "This torch has been lit for a hundred years, and we can't have you splashing water on it!"

"Is it the Torch of Peace, sir?" asked Leo. He stopped next to Tabby. "Is it true that it's really magical? Is it true that it keeps the peace among all kitizens, all through the land?"

"It most certainly is," replied Captain Edmund. "And it will travel with the king and queen on the royal boat."

Tabby's whiskers drooped. "I wish we could be on the boat," she said sadly. "Mom and Dad said we have to watch from the riverbank."

Captain Edmund ruffled her ears. "Cheer up, young Tabby. At least that rotten rat king, Gorgonzola, won't cause any trouble this time! I hear the Whiskered Wonders dunked him in a big bowl of cheese. The rascal's probably too ashamed to show his whiskers in Mewtopia ever again!"

At the mention of the Whiskered Wonders, Tabby and Leo shared a knowing look. *If only Captain Edmund knew the truth!*

"We have to go now," said Felix. "Nanny Mittens will be waiting for us."

"See you at the parade!" called Captain Edmund, and he marched off again with the torch held high.

Leo giggled as the royal kittens darted away, up the stairs to their bedchamber in the tallest tower in the palace. "Imagine what Captain Edmund would say if he knew that we *are* the Whiskered Wonders!" he said. "Secret heroes of Mewtopia!"

Leo and Felix gave each other a high paw, but Tabby was thinking of the wicked rat king, with his iron crown, greasy fur, and cruel yellow eyes. He would do anything to take over their kingdom. *I have a feeling that he won't let a bit of cheese get in his way . . .*

"Bless my whiskers!" gasped Nanny Mittens when the royal kittens finally reached their room. "You look like drowned mice! Well, never mind. You must all look your best for the Peace Parade. Get your towels, and quickly please!"

While Tabby and her brothers dried off, the big white cat picked out their nicest clothes and laid them on their baskets. Tabby saw that Nanny Mittens had brushed her whiskers and combed her fur. But she was still wearing her frilly apron.

"You haven't gotten dressed up yet, either, Nanny!" said Leo.

"My word, you're right!" Nanny Mittens swept out of the room, calling behind her.

"Into your clothes, my dears. The parade is about to begin!"

As soon as Nanny Mittens had closed the door, Tabby flung open their dress-up box. "We should put our Whiskered Wonders costumes on underneath," she said.

Felix nibbled his claws nervously. "Why? You don't think we'll need them at the Peace Parade, do you?"

"I hope not," said Tabby. "But I don't think we've seen the last of Gorgonzola. And if he tries to cause any trouble, we'll be ready for him!"

Chapter 2

PEACE PARADE

"Thank goodness for Nanny Mittens!" said King Pouncalot as Tabby and her brothers climbed into the royal carriage in the courtyard. "You kitties look perfect."

"*Almost* perfect," said Queen Elizapet. She licked her paw and scrubbed Leo's ears with it.

Tabby grinned as the carriage moved off. *Soon we'll be at the river!*

She patted her skirt carefully. She had hidden three swords under it, just in case. *But I hope we don't have to use them . . .*

The carriage rolled out of the palace and down the Royal Avenue. Kitizens crowded the street, cheering and clapping as they passed. Tabby's heart raced with excitement.

Then they turned a corner, and the kittens gasped. *The royal boat!* It was long and wooden, floating on the river, painted white and gold. A big red flag flew from the mast, showing the golden claws of Mewtopia.

The banks of the river were completely full of kitizens. They sat on picnic rugs, dressed in their best clothes, munching tuna sandwiches and sipping iced milk.

"They're all waiting for us!" said Leo, his tail flicking with excitement.

"And you must behave yourselves for them," said King Pouncalot, wagging a claw. "Royal kittens must set a good example for little kitties all over the kingdom."

At last the carriage door swung open.

"Greetings, kitizens!" called Queen Elizapet.

The royal family climbed down from the carriage. The kitizens leaped to their paws, clapping wildly and throwing colorful confetti.

Another carriage rolled up behind theirs. Nanny Mittens climbed out. She wore a green dress and a large pink hat shaped like a rose. Captain Edmund followed, proudly carrying the Torch of Peace. It was glowing brighter than ever.

All around, kitizens fell silent in amazement.

"It's the torch!" one whispered.

"Isn't it beautiful?" sighed another.

"I hope he doesn't drop it!" whispered Felix, nibbling his claws again.

Captain Edmund marched to the river, his armor shining in the light of the flames. Then he kneeled down.

Tabby and her brothers followed their parents to the edge of the water. King Pouncalot took the torch from Captain

Edmund. He held it up high, so that every cat could see it.

"Behold the Torch of Peace!" said Queen Elizapet. "May our celebration today bring all cats and kittens together. And may there be peace in Mewtopia . . . forever!"

Everyone cheered, and the king and queen bowed. Then they walked up a ramp onto the deck of the royal boat, followed by Captain Edmund. *I wish we were up there with them*, thought Tabby, her whiskers drooping.

King Pouncalot placed the Torch of Peace into a special holder at the front of the boat. Then he threw out his paws. "Let the Peace Parade begin!"

A brass band began to play, and the kitizens meowed excitedly.

Nanny Mittens got a picnic basket from her carriage. She laid out a checkered blanket on an empty spot of grass, and the royal kittens all sat cross-legged on top of it.

"There's one good thing about being

stuck on the bank," said Felix. "We get to see all the other boats in the parade!"

Sure enough, as the royal boat moved off, more boats came sailing behind it. The first was piled high with brightly colored balls of wool. The next was painted all white, and was a very strange shape.

"It's a milk bottle!" said Leo suddenly. "It's just lying on its side."

The royal kittens giggled at the sight. Nanny Mittens handed them each a little bag of tuna treats, and Tabby began to feel much better. She could see her parents on the deck of the royal boat, smiling and waving. She waved back.

"That boat looks even funnier than the milk bottle," said Felix.

Tabby looked down the river and saw a huge yellow lump floating on the water.

Nanny Mittens frowned. "It looks like a big smelly cheese boat!"

Cheese . . . Tabby felt a shiver run down

her tail. She looked at her brothers. Leo frowned, and Felix started to bite his claws again.

"You don't think..." whispered Felix. "It can't be..."

"King Gorgonzola?" finished Leo.

Tabby stared hard at the boat. It really was made out of cheese, with sails of white mozzarella, and cheddar cannons poking out on both sides. A black flag was flying from the mast. On it was a picture of some white cheese, speckled with blue. *Oh no...*

"I'd know that cheese anywhere," said Tabby. "It's gorgonzola!"

She looked at the deck. A rat stood there, wearing a torn gray cape and an iron crown. He was grinning, showing off his rotten yellow teeth.

It's King Gorgonzola!

Chapter 3

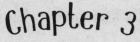

SAY CHEESE

"Open fire!" yelled Gorgonzola.

Three more rats on the cheese ship rushed to the cannons. Tabby knew who they were at once.

"It's Chedd, Brie, and Mozz," said Felix.

"Gorgonzola's rat servants!" added Leo.

"Say cheese!" shouted Mozz from aboard the ship.

SPLOOSH! SPLOOSH! SPLOOSH!

Three balls of gloopy cheese shot from the cannons.

SPLAT! The first hit the wool boat, rocking it in the water. *SPLOSH!* The second splattered all over the milk bottle boat. *SPLURGE!* The third dripped down the side of the royal boat.

"Our beautiful boat!" cried King Pouncalot.

"Crooks!" yelled Captain Edmund, shaking a paw. "Pirates! Cheese lovers!"

Wails went up from the kitizens on the bank. "Rats!" someone yelled. "They're ruining the Peace Parade!"

"Oh my whiskers," gasped Nanny Mittens. She fanned herself with her program. "This is all too much! I feel so faint . . ."

Tabby gave her brothers a look. She knew they were all thinking the same thing. *Mewtopia needs the Whiskered Wonders again!* But first they had to help Nanny Mittens— and then get out from under her watchful eye.

"This way, Nanny Mittens," Tabby said. "There's a tent over there."

"You can sit down with a nice cup of tea," said Felix.

"Just follow us!" said Leo.

Together, the royal kittens helped Nanny Mittens to her paws. Then they guided her through the crowds. Everyone was looking in horror at the cheese ship as it sailed closer to the royal boat . . .

"We'll be back soon," Tabby said as they sat Nanny Mittens down on a chair in the tent. "We're just going to check on Mom and Dad."

"That's nice, my dears," said Nanny Mittens faintly. "I'm sure some tea will make me feel much better."

Felix got Nanny Mittens a cup of tea, then the royal kittens hurried out and around to the back of the tent.

Quickly they pulled off their fancy clothes to reveal their costumes. Felix passed around the masks, while Tabby handed out the swords. In a few moments they were

ready, all dressed in black with their masks
tied on—a red mask for Tabby, a purple one
for Felix, and a green one for Leo.

"Time to save Mewtopia again," said Leo,
swishing his sword through the air. "The
Whiskered Wonders are on the case!"

They rushed out and hurried to the edge
of the water. Gasps rose up all around.

"It's the Whiskered Wonders!"

"They've come to save us!"

"Make way, everyone!"

Tabby felt a buzz of excitement, and her tail swished. She felt like a real hero, like Silverpaw from the adventure stories that Nanny Mittens read them before bedtime. *The kitizens are all counting on us! We can't let them down . . .*

As they reached the river, Tabby saw that Gorgonzola's cheese ship was now right next to the royal boat. *SPLOOSH! SPLOOSH!* More cheesy cannonballs shot through the air and splattered onto the boat. Tabby's parents were hiding by the mast, with Captain Edmund bravely standing in front of them. Another cannonball hit the deck, splattering Queen Elizapet's dress with cheese . . .

"Leaping fleas!" cried Felix. He was staring at the river. "How are we going to get to Mom and Dad?"

Tabby looked all around, but there were no boats tied up by the bank.

"The boats are all on the water!" said Leo.

"Wait . . ." said Tabby. She pointed to a boat sailing very close to the bank, which was square and painted to look like a tin of sardines. "We can jump to that one. Then to the next one along . . ."

"Like stepping stones!" said Leo.

"Great idea, Tabby," said Felix. "Let's go! One . . . two . . . three . . ."

The royal kittens all jumped at the same time. They landed on the sardine boat, and Tabby felt it wobble in the water. She held out her tail for balance. *Made it!*

"That one next," said Tabby. She pointed to a boat that had round ears at the front and a tail at the back, like a mouse.

The royal kittens jumped again, and landed safely on the mouse boat.

"Just one more," said Leo, pointing to a boat with an enormous scratching post instead of a mast. "Then we can jump to the royal boat!"

"It's too far," said Felix, frowning. He

pointed up to the mast of the mouse boat, where a rope hung. "I think we have to swing."

"We'll be just like Silverpaw!" said Leo, grinning as he climbed up the mast. He took hold of the rope. "One . . . two . . . THREE!"

Leo kicked away from the mast and swung across the water. Then he let go and dropped down onto the deck of the next boat.

Felix went next, and then it was Tabby's turn. *I'm very high up*, she thought. Then she took a deep breath and kicked away from the mast. "For Mewtopia!" she called. In midair she let go, landing safely on the scratching-post boat.

"Phew!" gasped Tabby. "Look, there's Mom and Dad. But they're covered in cheese!"

Only a few feet away on the royal boat, King Pouncalot and Queen Elizapet were stuck to the mast by big globs of cheese from the cannons. "Guards!" shouted King Pouncalot. But the soldiers were just as stuck. Tabby saw Captain Edmund trying to draw his sword, but it was glued to his belt with melted cheese. *There's cheese everywhere!*

"Prepare to be boarded!" shouted King Gorgonzola. He jumped onto the boat, followed by Chedd, Brie, and Mozz. The rat servants pulled down the flag of Mewtopia. In its place, they raised a black flag with a lump of gorgonzola on it, just like the one on the cheese ship.

"This is my boat now!" yelled King Gorgonzola. "And I'm taking that torch."

"No!" shouted Captain Edmund. "Not the Torch of Peace!" He tried to run, but his paws were stuck to the deck with even more melted cheese.

"Whiskered Wonders!" cried Queen Elizapet as she spotted the royal kittens. "Please, save our torch!"

Gorgonzola looked over at the kittens. "Come to try to stop me again?" he said with an evil grin. "Well, you're too late!" With that, he ran to the front of the boat and pulled the torch from its holder. Then he threw it overboard.

"Noooo!" cried Tabby.

Splash! The torch hit the water. The magical flames went out with a hiss, and the torch started to sink. A moment later, it was gone.

A great cry rose up from the banks of the river. King Pouncalot and Queen Elizapet hung their heads.

"Ha-ha!" laughed Gorgonzola. "That's what I think of your silly torch! Now there'll be no more peace in Mewtopia! Even you whiskered wimps will be so busy arguing, you won't be able to stop me from taking over the kingdom!"

Tabby's heart sank even faster than the torch.

What if he's right . . . ?

Chapter 4

RAPIDS!

"There's nothing to worry about," said King Pouncalot. "The goldsmith will make a new Torch of Peace!"

"A new one?" said Queen Elizapet. "That's no good at all! We must get the old one back."

"We can't do that," snapped King Pouncalot. "We're stuck in all this cheese!"

Tabby could hardly believe her ears. "Mom and Dad are arguing!"

"No, they're not," said Felix. "It's just a disagreement."

"Why didn't you three catch the torch?" huffed Captain Edmund, looking at the three kittens. He was still struggling to move. "Whiskered Wonders, indeed . . . You're supposed to be heroes, aren't you?"

"You didn't catch it, either!" said Leo.

Everyone's arguing, thought Tabby. Even on the bank, she could see kitizens talking angrily, hissing, arching their backs, and waving their paws around. *It must be because the torch has gone out!*

King Gorgonzola stood at the front of the boat, rubbing his claws together and laughing with his rat servants. "I'll make Mewtopia part of Rottingham," he said. "Then these horribly cuddly kitties will all walk the plank. Go get it right now, Brie!"

"Yes, Your Stinkyness!" said Brie, bowing low. She dashed off to the cheese ship and came back with a wooden plank.

"And I'm going to get those Whiskered Wonders!" shouted Chedd. The kittens watched as he leaped off the side of the royal boat, but their scratching-post boat had drifted away, far out of reach. Chedd fell straight into the water. Then he splashed around, shaking his paw, and climbed back onto the royal boat.

"We have to stop this!" Tabby said to her brothers. "Gorgonzola *wants* us to argue."

"No, he doesn't!" said Leo angrily. Then he frowned. "Oh. Maybe you're right . . ."

"We'll just have to try really hard to get along," said Tabby. "Everyone else is too busy arguing to fix this! It's up to the Whiskered Wonders again."

"But where's the torch?" said Felix.

The royal kittens stared hard into the water. The river was deep, dark, and blue. Then . . .

"Look!" gasped Leo. "Is that a flash of gold?"

"It's a fish," said Felix.

"No!" said Tabby. "It's the Torch of Peace!"

"I really don't think . . ." Felix began. Then he clapped his paws over his mouth. "Sorry! You're probably right. Let's go after it!"

"The river's carrying it away," said Leo. "We need a boat of our own. Something faster than this!"

"Or three little boats," said Tabby. "Look!"

She pointed to a large boat close by, shaped like a big comfy cat basket, with a red blanket inside. Tied to its back were several mini life baskets, each just big enough for a kitten.

"Perfect!" said Felix.

The royal kittens hopped over to the big

basket, then jumped down into three of the little ones. They each drew their sword. *Swish!* They sliced through the ropes, and the boats drifted free. Tabby found an oar in her basket and began to paddle it like a canoe, away from the parade. She looked back and saw her brothers following her.

Every now and then, Tabby caught a glimpse of gold in the water up ahead. The torch was flowing fast with the river.

Soon she began to pant. *This is harder than it looks!* And the river was getting rougher, the water bubbling and foaming. They were pulled around a corner. Tabby glanced back to see the royal boat and the other boats disappear from view. *We're on our own now . . .*

The river carried them through the town, then—*swoosh!*—down the hillside. The water flowed faster and faster. Tabby gave a little yelp of fear. She pulled up her oar and held on tight with her claws.

"I don't like this!" wailed Felix.

Leo shouted back. "Don't be such a scaredy— Eeeek!"

The kittens began to bump and bounce up and down in their baskets. Tabby waved her tail for balance. Her fur stood on end. *Splash!* A wave of cold water soaked her to the skin.

"Oh my whiskers!" cried Leo. "I'm wet!"

"Not again!" moaned Felix.

Then Tabby saw it—a flash of gold, right beside her basket. She reached out to grab it . . .

SPLASH! A giant wave sent her tumbling from her basket. She fell deep into the river, heart racing. A moment later, she bobbed up, gasping and spitting out water. She saw Felix and Leo also splashing in the water nearby. The river was white and foaming, and the baskets had disappeared.

"Rapids!" called Felix. "Help!"

Tabby was being pulled along, but there was nothing she could do to stop it. The river was flowing too fast and strong.

"Look!" yelled Leo, his yellow eyes wide.

Tabby's heart pounded harder than ever. Ahead the river curved sharply around groups of big rocks. *What's on the other side?*

She felt Felix's paw close around hers. She reached out and grabbed Leo's paw, too. "We're heading for the rocks!" she yelled. "Hold on tight!"

Chapter 5

FISHING FOR GOLD

Whoooosh!

The kittens went swirling just past the rocks, around the bend in the river, then came to a gentle stop.

"I can't look!" said Felix. He was kitty-paddling, with his eyes tightly shut. "Is it a waterfall?"

Tabby grinned. "It's a lake!"

Sure enough, the three royal kittens

were floating in a huge, calm circle of water. It was as smooth as a mirror, and trees surrounded its banks.

"What are you kitties waiting for?" said Leo. "I'm getting out of here!"

The three of them splashed their way to the bank and climbed out. Tabby shook herself, and water flew from her fur. The sun was warm. She could feel it drying her already. Leo had a weed hanging over one ear, and she picked it off.

"I'm never getting in water again," said Felix, his ears drooping. "Not even for a bath!"

"Good luck telling Nanny Mittens that," said Tabby. "Anyway, we *have* to go in. The torch must have sunk to the bottom of the lake. We need to find it."

They stared into the water. It looked very deep and dark, and none of them could see the bottom.

"Well, I definitely can't get it," said Leo. "I'm too little."

"No, you're not," said Tabby. "Being little means you can wiggle through the weeds more easily."

"But you saw the torch last, Tabby," said Felix. "So you should go in and get it."

That's not fair, Tabby was about to say. Then she shook her head. "We're arguing again! We'll never get the torch back this way."

"And Gorgonzola will take over Mewtopia," said Felix.

"That ratbag!" said Leo. "We have to try to get along with one another, no matter what."

"Agreed!" said Tabby.

Felix stroked his whiskers. "If nobody will go into the water, how do we get the torch back?"

The kittens fell silent, all thinking hard.

Tabby saw a flicker of silver near the surface of the water. For a moment she thought it was the torch, but it was only a fish. *Hang on a minute . . .*

"Fishercats!" she said.

"Bless you," said Felix.

"No!" Tabby pointed into the water. "There are fish in the lake. So there are probably fishercats somewhere nearby. Maybe they could help fish out the torch!"

Leo hopped up and down with excitement. "That's perfect! Let's go!"

The little orange cat ran off, and Tabby and Felix followed. They hurried along the bank, around the edge of the lake.

As they pushed through the trees, Tabby spotted a little group of houses by a sandy beach. Her heart leaped. There were fishing rods by each house's door, and the wooden roofs had nets strung over them. There were little boats, too. Some were pulled up on the sand, while others bobbed in the water.

A pair of kittens in matching yellow pants sat on the beach, fixing a net. As the royal kittens got closer, Tabby realized the fisherkittens were arguing.

"You threw it too far!" said one. "That's why it ripped."

"We were too close to the rocks," said the other. "You should have steered the boat away!"

"Oh no!" whispered Felix. "They're arguing here, too!"

"You fix it then, if you're so smart!" shouted the first cat. He stood and stomped off back to the village.

His friend sighed and put down the net. She was a slim white cat with a black face and ears.

"Hello there," said Tabby, waving a paw.

The kitten turned, and her fur fluffed up with shock. "Sweet catnip! It's the Whiskered Wonders!" She blinked her big blue eyes. "We've heard all about you. You're so brave, saving Mewtopia from King Gorgonzola!"

"Nice to meet you," said Leo, twirling his tail. "I suppose we are pretty brave!"

"I'm Suki," said the fisherkitten. "What brings you to our little village?"

"Actually, we need some help . . ."

Tabby quickly explained about the Torch

of Peace, how Gorgonzola had thrown it into the river, and how they'd followed it.

"So you see, we really need to get it back," she finished.

Suki shook her head in surprise. "No wonder! I've never argued with Nico before. We're best friends!"

"So will you help us find the torch?" asked Felix.

"Of course!" said Suki. "Actually, some fishercats just came back from the lake. Let's see if they've caught it in their nets."

Suki led them over the beach to three big nets full of fish.

Leo's tummy rumbled. "Those fish look yummy!" he said, licking his lips.

"No time to eat!" said Felix. "We've got to find the Torch of Peace, remember?"

Leo groaned and rubbed his belly.

The four kittens opened the nets, then sat on the sand, digging with their paws among the slippery silver fish. But there was no hint of gold anywhere.

"It's not here!" said Tabby at last.

"I could take you out in my boat?" offered Suki. "We could fish for it ourselves."

Felix twitched his tail anxiously. "Thanks, Suki. But that could take a long time, couldn't it? The water is too deep to see what's on the bottom."

Suki frowned. "Actually, that gives me an idea . . . Wait here!"

The royal kittens watched her run into a little house by the jetty. A wooden fish hung over the door with HOME SWEET HOME painted on it.

A moment later, Suki came back out with her arms full. Tabby saw that she was carrying three strange outfits. They were made of bulky brass and thick red rubber that covered the whole body, and all four paws, too. Each outfit had a round glass helmet, like a fishbowl.

"They're diving suits," panted Suki. She gave one to each of the royal kittens. "They let you breathe underwater. And you can even talk to one another through the helmets."

Tabby shared a nervous look with her brothers.

"You mean we have to go to the bottom of the lake by ourselves?" said Leo.

"I'd come with you," Suki said, "but there are only three suits. Anyway, one of us should stay up here, in case you get in trouble."

"Trouble?" said Felix. He was already

nibbling at his claws. "Oh my whiskers. Can we think about it?"

Suki nodded. "Of course!"

The royal kittens huddled together.

"Do we have to do this?" asked Felix.

"At least with those suits we won't get wet," said Tabby, trying to sound as brave as she could. "And if we don't hurry up and find that torch, King Gorgonzola will take over the kingdom!"

"Tabby's right," said Leo. "Let's do it. For Mewtopia!"

Felix sighed. "Well, in that case, I guess I'm coming, too."

Tabby turned to Suki. "We all agree," she said. "We're going in!"

Chapter 6

THE MYSTERIOUS TUNNEL

Click! Suki fitted Tabby's glass helmet onto the brass neck piece.

"There!" she said, stepping back. "All done. You look great!"

Tabby frowned. "I feel like my head's stuck in a fishbowl!"

"You look like it, too," said Leo, grinning.

Tabby couldn't help grinning back. Felix and Leo were sitting on the dock in their diving gear. Their diving suits reminded Tabby of the suits of armor that stood in the halls of the palace back home. *A home we'll lose, if Gorgonzola gets his way!*

"Good luck," said Suki. "Oh—and look out for the tangleweed."

"What's that?" asked Felix, his green eyes wide. "It sounds dangerous!"

But Leo was already climbing down into the water. "Come on!" he yelled. "We've got a torch to find!"

Tabby and Felix shared a nervous look.

"On three," said Tabby. "One . . . two . . . THREE!"

SPLASH! They both jumped in.

Tabby sank quickly under the water. Her

heart beat hard, but this time she couldn't feel the horrible cold wetness on her fur. Instead the water pressed against her suit, as though her whole body was wrapped in a gentle hug.

The lake looked blue and foggy. It was strangely silent. Tabby realized she was holding her breath, and let it out. *These suits let us breathe normally, even down here!* She could see her brothers next to her, looking around in astonishment. *Maybe going underwater isn't so bad after all.*

They all landed on their paws on the lake bed.

"Meowza!" said Leo. "This is so cool!"

"I think it's creepy!" said Felix with a

shiver. "Kittens are supposed to stay on land, if you ask me."

Tabby could just hear their voices, which sounded quieter in the water.

"Come on," she said. "For Mewtopia!"

They set off slowly. It was hard having to push their legs through the water with each step, and Tabby was soon tired. The rocky ground dropped down as they headed for the middle of the lake.

Now and then, Tabby saw a school of fish burst through the water. Their brightly colored scales flickered, catching the light from above. *They look so beautiful down here!* But when she looked into the shadows beyond, she couldn't help feeling a squirm of fear.

"I don't like this at all," whispered Felix. "Who knows what lives down here?"

Just then, something long and silver shot in front of them, leaving a trail of bubbles.

The royal kittens stopped. "What was that?" asked Leo.

Whoosh! The creature swam past again, closer this time. Tabby saw a big silver eye and shiny teeth. Then it disappeared into the shadows.

"It's an eel!" yelled Felix. "Swim for your lives!"

The royal kittens began to paddle quickly with their paws. *Do eels eat kittens?* Tabby's heart raced. She really didn't want to find out.

"It's coming back!" cried Leo.

Tabby looked over her shoulder. Sure enough, the eel was coming after them. Its body wiggled from side to side. It was so long she couldn't see the end of its tail, and its mouth was open wide.

The royal kittens swam even faster—as fast as they could.

"It's going to get me!" shouted Leo.

Uh-oh . . . Tabby saw that her little brother was struggling. His paws were smaller than hers and Felix's, and he couldn't swim as fast. He was puffing and panting already.

"We can't escape it," wailed Felix.

"Then we'll have to hide!" said Tabby.

She looked all around. *There!* On the

lake bed below, she saw a thick patch of green weeds.

"Follow me!" called Tabby. She dived down, straight into the weeds. Swimming through them, she hid on the lake bed, completely covered. A moment later, Felix and Leo came floating down next to her.

They waited and waited. No one said a word.

"Do you think it's gone?" asked Felix, at last.

Slowly, carefully, Tabby lifted her head up above the weeds. In the distance, she saw a flash of the eel's silver tail as it swam off. *Phew!* "We're safe," she told the others. "Thank goodness!"

"Let's get out of here, before it comes back!" said Felix.

But when Tabby tried to move her back paw, something was holding it tight. She tried her other back paw. But that was stuck, too.

"The weeds!" said Leo. "They've got my paws!"

Suddenly, Tabby remembered Suki's warning. *Tangleweed! We were so busy trying to escape from the eel, we forgot all about it!*

"No wonder that eel didn't follow us down here," said Felix. "It didn't want to get stuck."

Tabby twisted and turned, trying to get her leg free. But the weeds only seemed to hold her more tightly. She tried her other paw, but that was no good, either. She bent over to tug at the weeds, but they wouldn't come off.

This is hopeless!

"We shouldn't have hidden here!" said Felix crossly. "This is your fault, Tabby."

"There was nowhere else to hide!"

snapped Tabby. "Anyway, it's Leo's fault for being such a slow swimmer. If he hadn't—" She stopped. "Leaping fleas, we're arguing again!"

Felix slapped a paw to his helmet. "You're right! Sorry, Tabby."

"I'm sorry, too," said Tabby. "It's not your fault, Leo."

"Let's just get out of these weeds," said Leo. "I don't like being stuck underwater!"

"I've got an idea," said Felix. "We're not strong enough to get ourselves out on our own, but maybe if we work together . . ."

"We could get one paw free at a time!" finished Tabby. "Great idea, Felix! Let's start with Leo."

Tabby and Felix bent over to help Leo. Together, they all tugged at the weed around his back-left paw. They pulled, and pulled, and . . .

Pop! All of a sudden, his leg came free. Leo pulled up his paw, rubbing at it. "Yes!" he cried. "Now let's do the other one!"

They freed Leo's other back paw. Then they pulled the weeds from Felix.

Tabby went last. As soon as she had her paws free, she paddled out of the weeds, and the three of them climbed onto a rocky patch of the lake bed. "That feels so much better!" said Tabby. "Now, where's that Torch of Peace?"

"I think I see something!" said Felix. His whiskers were shaking with excitement as he stared into the shadowy blue of the water. "Just down there."

Tabby's heart leaped. She saw it, too—a distant sparkle of gold.

"That has to be the torch!" yelled Leo, swishing his tail. "Last one there is a grumpy crab!"

The royal kittens swam as fast as they could. As they came closer, they saw the gold was shining from the rocks beside a cave. The entrance was so dark they couldn't see a thing inside.

Tabby reached down between the rocks,

but her heart sank again as she pulled out the golden object.

"Whoa!" said Felix. "It's not the torch at all. It's our toy boat!"

He was right. Amazingly, the clockwork boat didn't have a dent on it.

"It must have floated all the way down the river after we lost it," said Leo. "I can't believe it!"

Tabby sighed. *I was so sure it was the Torch of Peace!* She passed the boat to Leo, who wrapped it up in a bit of seaweed, then tied it onto the belt of his diving suit.

"Are you all right, Tabby?" asked Felix. "You're frowning."

Tabby blinked and nodded. "Sorry! I was just thinking . . . If the river carried our boat down here, maybe it carried the torch somewhere nearby, too."

The kittens all turned together to stare into the cave. Tabby felt the fur stand up at the back of her neck.

"Do you think it went in there?" whispered Leo.

Felix sighed. "I guess there's only one way to find out."

Tabby nodded. She could feel her tail twitching nervously. *That cave looks scary! But we have to find that torch.*

"I'll go first," said Leo.

The little orange cat swam into the cave.

"Wait for us!" called Felix as he and Tabby followed.

Inside the cave, it was almost completely black. Tabby's heart thumped. She could just see rocks on either side as they swam in. But the cave seemed to go on forever, getting even darker as they swam farther in. Tabby glanced back, and felt a lump in her throat. She couldn't see the entrance anymore.

"I don't think this is a cave at all," said Felix's voice from somewhere close by. "I think it's a tunnel."

"If it's a tunnel, it must lead somewhere," said Tabby. *But where?*

They turned a corner, and a blue light glowed on the rocks ahead. *It must be the way out!* Tabby swam faster. She passed Felix and Leo. Then she swam out into a huge, open space.

Meowza!

Tabby could hardly believe what she was seeing.

She was in an underground room, with blue crystals shining from the ceiling. Far below, there was a strange-looking little village, built on the rocks. And swimming in the water around it were the oddest creatures Tabby had ever seen. They flashed through the water, flicking huge silver-green fish tails. *But each one has the body of a cat!*

"Oh my whiskers," gasped Leo as he and Felix arrived next to Tabby. "Catfish!"

Chapter 7

CATFISH KINGDOM

Tabby had read about catfish in her adventure books. *But I didn't think they were real!* She watched in amazement as they darted and dived through the water.

"Let's go and say hi!" said Leo. "Maybe they know where the torch went."

The royal kittens swam down toward the village.

As they got closer, Tabby saw that the

houses were made of wood and shaped like boats. Soft yellow light shone from round windows onto little gardens, full of coral and shells. Here and there, glowing jellyfish floated between the houses like streetlights. *It's so pretty!*

A crowd of catfish had gathered around a statue of a ship in the middle of the village. It was made of gray stone, with white marble sails. But the statue was cracked in half.

Catfish voices drifted through the water toward them.

"Don't look at me! I didn't break it!"

"Well, it wasn't me, either!"

"*Someone* must have done it!"

Tabby looked at her brothers. "Uh-oh. They're arguing down here, too! We *really* need to find that torch."

"I wonder why they have a statue of a ship?" said Felix.

Leo shrugged. "Their houses all look like boats, too. They must really like them!"

Just then, a catfish looked up and saw the kittens. His big blue eyes went wide, and he pointed with a webbed paw. "Land cats!"

"It was them!" shouted another catfish. "They came down here to break our statue!"

"Wait, you've got it wrong!" said Felix.

But it was too late. The whole crowd of catfish came rushing toward them. Strong paws grabbed Tabby by both arms and legs. She struggled, but she couldn't get free.

"Come on!" said a blue catfish wearing a pearl necklace. "Let's take these horrible land kittens to the queen. She'll know just what to do with them!"

"I don't like the sound of this," whispered Felix as the catfish began to swim. But there was nothing they could do. The kittens were dragged through the water, held tightly by the catfish. *Where are they taking us?* wondered Tabby. *I didn't know they had a queen . . .* She licked her whiskers nervously.

The blue catfish led the way through the village, until they reached a building shaped like a huge ship. It was taller than all the other houses, and covered in bright white shells. The blue catfish swam in through a large, round door, and the other catfish pulled the royal kittens in after her.

"Whoa!" gasped Leo.

Inside, the ship was completely hollow. The walls and floor glittered with shiny bits of coral and shells. At the very end of the room was a white coral throne. Two catfish guards floated beside it, each holding a sharp spear.

Sitting in the throne was an old white catfish with a very long silver tail. She was wearing a seaweed robe and a crown made of pebbles and shells. *She looks a bit like*

Nanny Mittens, thought Tabby. *But not as nice . . . and with more scales!*

The queen's orange eyes narrowed when she saw the royal kittens. "Land cats!" she hissed. "What are you doing in my waters?"

"They really don't like us, do they?" whispered Felix.

Tabby frowned. *I wonder why not?*

The catfish holding Tabby's arms and legs finally let go. Tabby saw that he and the other catfish were all bowing to the queen. Quickly she and her brothers did the same.

"Greetings, Your Meowjesty," said Tabby.

The catfish queen raised an eyebrow.

"Well, at least they have some manners," she said. "I am Queen Pearl. And you are?"

"We're the Whiskered Wonders," said Leo.

But before he could say anything else, the blue catfish swam forward. "They broke our statue, Oh Watery One!"

The queen's tail flicked with anger. "Is that true?"

"No!" said all three royal kittens at once.

"But it's no wonder you've been arguing about it," said Tabby.

She felt a little nervous to see all the catfish staring at her, but she forced herself to keep going. "The evil rat, King Gorgonzola, attacked our Peace Parade. Then he threw the Torch of Peace in the river. The torch has gone out, so cats are arguing with one another everywhere, on land and in the water!"

Queen Pearl was looking thoughtful. "A Torch of Peace, you say? Does it look like this?" She reached behind her throne and pulled out something. A shining, golden rod . . .

"That's it!" said Leo. He paddled his paws with excitement, drifting up off the floor.

"I *knew* it was some sort of land cat nonsense," said Queen Pearl. The other catfish all nodded in agreement. "The river carried it here," the queen continued. "I think I'm going to use it as a rolling pin, to make seaweed cookies."

"You can't!" shouted Tabby, swimming forward.

Queen Pearl frowned. The catfish guards pointed their spears at Tabby.

Tabby stopped, her whiskers shaking with fear. *But I have to make her understand!* "We need to light it again!" she explained. "If we don't, all the arguments will keep going forever."

"And King Gorgonzola will take over Mewtopia," added Felix.

Queen Pearl blew a raspberry. "Why should I care about that? Land cats don't care about us!"

"What do you mean?" asked Felix.

"Well, I suppose you're too young to

know," said Queen Pearl, looking down her nose at him. "A long time ago, the catfish used to come to your Peace Parades. Then the land cats stopped inviting us!"

"We loved the parade," said the blue catfish. "So many boats! All different shapes and sizes."

"We *love* boats!" said Queen Pearl, and all the catfish purred in agreement. "And we *really* loved building a special boat every year to go in the Peace Parade. It was the best day of the year! Now we just stay down here all the time."

The catfish hung their heads sadly.

Tabby frowned. *I can't believe Mom and Dad wouldn't invite the catfish!* She thought about how disappointed she was when they told her she and her brothers couldn't ride on the royal boat earlier today. *No wonder the catfish are so upset.* But there had to be a reason.

"I'm sure the land cats—I mean we—just forgot to invite you!" said Tabby. "In fact, we would love it if you would come to the Peace Parade."

"It's horrible feeling left out," added Leo.

"Hmm," said Queen Pearl. "It would be a shame to lose my new rolling pin . . ."

"We can't trust these land cats, Oh Watery One!" hissed the blue catfish. "What if it's a trick?"

"We promise it's not!" said Felix.

"And I can prove it," said Leo suddenly. Tabby and Felix both turned to look at him. Leo unwrapped the seaweed at his belt and held out something small and golden. *The toy boat!*

The catfish crowded around, purring louder in amazement. Even Queen Pearl swam off her throne to stare at it. Her orange eyes were open wide. "It's beautiful!"

"Look at the little sails!" gasped the blue catfish.

"And the tiny anchor," added Queen Pearl.

"This is our favorite toy," said Leo. "But we'd like you to have it. So you know that we really do want to be friends." He took a deep breath and held out the boat.

"Good job, Leo," whispered Tabby. She knew how much the boat meant to her brother, and she was proud of him for giving it away.

"So can we be friends?" asked Felix.

Queen Pearl carefully took the golden boat from Leo's paws. "You know, our ship statue is really very old," she said thoughtfully. "That's probably why it cracked."

"We're sorry we blamed you," said the blue catfish.

Tabby grinned. "We don't mind," she said. "We're just glad the land cats and the catfish are friends again!"

"And we are, too," said Queen Pearl. She smiled and held out the Torch of Peace.

"You may take this back to the parade now."

Felix reached for the torch, but Tabby put a paw on his arm. "Hang on," she said. "I think I just had an idea! Oh Watery One, could you please look after the torch for a little longer?"

Queen Pearl looked surprised, but she nodded. "Of course, my dear."

"But then everyone will keep arguing!" said Felix.

"Exactly!" said Tabby. Her whiskers shook with excitement. "Just wait and see. I think I know how to defeat King Gorgonzola!"

Chapter 8

A TASTY SHIP

Soon afterward, the royal kittens were back in the fresh air. They were sailing up the river on a fishing boat they had borrowed from Suki after they returned the diving suits. Felix was steering, while Leo leaned over the front, twitching his tail eagerly.

As they rowed back into the town, Tabby took a deep breath. It felt good to be out of the diving suits and above the water. But she couldn't relax. *We don't have much time to stop Gorgonzola!*

"I see it!" yelled Felix suddenly, hopping up and down. "I see the royal boat!"

They went around a bend in the river, and Tabby turned to see the Peace Parade come into view. *But it doesn't look very peaceful at all!* On the riverbank, the kitizens were all still shouting at one another. On the water, boats were drifting here and there, as the sailors were too busy arguing to steer them. *It's worse than ever!*

Gorgonzola's cheese ship was bobbing next to the royal boat. Tabby could see her parents and Captain Edmund, sitting tied up by the mast.

"Nonsense!" Queen Elizapet was saying crossly. "My crown is far prettier."

"But mine has rubies in it!" snapped King Pouncalot.

"They're both silly, if you ask me," huffed Captain Edmund. "Look how silver my armor is!"

"I don't believe it," said Leo, his eyes wide. "They're acting like spoiled little kitties!"

"It's all Gorgonzola's fault," said Felix. "And look—he's brought more rats!"

Sure enough, Tabby saw King Gorgonzola standing at the front of the royal boat, with a big crowd of rats around him. He was pointing with his claws, giving them orders. "Raise the anchor!" he squeaked. "Set sail for the palace! Mewtopia will soon be mine . . . I mean, ours!"

"He hasn't noticed us yet," said Tabby. "If we're quick, maybe we can sneak onto the boat."

Felix steered their little boat closer, until it bumped gently against the side of the royal boat. The royal kittens scrambled out. They used their claws to pull themselves onto the deck. Then they ducked down behind a big barrel. Peeking out, Tabby saw the rats hurrying around the deck, following Gorgonzola's orders. There was Brie, pulling on a rope. Chedd and Mozz were rolling a barrel across the deck.

"Now what?" whispered Leo.

"Now we try my plan," said Tabby, trying to sound confident. *I really hope this works!*

She made her voice sound squeaky, like a rat. "Brie's tail is so stumpy!" she shouted.

Brie spun around. "Who said that?"

"Not me!" said Chedd.

"Good," said Brie. "Because you hardly have a tail at all!"

Tabby grinned. *It's working!*

Leo shouted out in a rat voice, too. "Mozz smells like yucky flowers!"

Some of the rats turned to look at Mozz.

He curled up his tail in embarrassment. "It's my new perfume!" he said.

Soon the rats were all fighting with one another.

"My armpits are stinkier than anyone's!"

"No, mine are!"

"My teeth are the most rotten!"

"Nonsense!" screamed King Gorgonzola. "Mine are so rotten they could fall out any minute!"

As the rats fought, Felix gave Tabby a high paw. "Great plan!" he whispered.

"And now for the most important part . . ." said Tabby. She cupped her paws around her mouth and shouted again in her rat voice.

"I can eat more cheese than any of you!"

"Who dares say that?" screeched King Gorgonzola. "I eat a mountain of cheese every day!"

"I eat *two* mountains, just for breakfast!" yelled Brie.

"You couldn't even eat half a block," scoffed Chedd. "*I* eat so much cheese I'm turning yellow!"

"You don't even like cheese!" snapped Mozz.

"Cheese-eating contest!" shouted Tabby, as squeakily as she could. "Everyone onto the cheese ship!"

Yelling and pushing, the rats ran across the deck of the royal boat. They leaped over the water, onto their own ship. Then they began to eat. Some bit chunks from the cheddar cannons. Some pulled down the mozzarella sails and stuffed them in their mouths. Others snatched at the stringcheese rigging, and slurped it up like spaghetti.

"They're eating their own ship!" giggled Leo.

Tabby punched the air in triumph. *Just like I planned!*

Only King Gorgonzola had stayed on the royal boat. "Wait!" he screamed. "You're going to sink it! Get back here and set sail for the palace! Stop eating that tasty ship!"

"He's just jealous," said Mozz, in between mouthfuls. "He can't eat as much cheese as we can!"

"Now's our chance!" whispered Felix.

While King Gorgonzola hopped up and down, yelling and shaking his claws, the royal kittens snuck out from behind the barrel. Quickly, they ran to the mast. They cut Captain Edmund free with their swords, then the king and queen.

"Thank you, Whiskered Wonders!" gasped Queen Elizapet, smoothing down her robe.

"You saved us!" added King Pouncalot, straightening his crown.

"Shh!" Tabby held a paw to her lips. Then she ran across the deck. The guards were tied up there at the other end of the ship, and she set them free, too.

"Nooooo!" wailed King Gorgonzola.

Tabby saw that he was still staring at the cheese ship, tugging his ears in fury. The rats had nibbled so many holes in the cheese that the ship was sinking, and fast. Bubbles sprang up all around it, and rats began to dive into the water. The river carried them away, tails waving, paws scrabbling.

"Good-bye!" said Leo. "Write us a postcard. Or not!"

"Hold on," said Felix, nibbling his claws nervously. "If all the rats are over there . . . Who's steering the royal boat?"

CRAAAAASH!

The royal kittens went tumbling, head

over tail. The whole boat had stopped still. When Tabby scrambled up, she saw that it had hit the bank.

"Uh-oh . . ." said Leo as the deck started to tilt. "I think the royal boat is sinking, too!"

"Everybody off!" shouted Captain Edmund. "Onto dry land!"

Tabby found the wooden plank that Brie had brought from the cheese ship. She placed one end on the bank, and the other on the deck. "This way!" she called. "Remember, Gorgonzola said we were going to walk the plank . . . and now we will! Follow the Whiskered Wonders!"

The royal kittens ran across the plank

onto the grassy bank, followed by the king and queen, Captain Edmund, and the guards—after they had finished arguing about who went first.

Tabby looked back at the royal boat. It was going down fast now. But as the back end sank below the water, she saw a single figure clinging to the front.

King Gorgonzola still had his gray cape wrapped around him, but his iron crown was hanging half off his head. He spotted Tabby. The fury in his yellow eyes sent a shiver of fear through her, right to the tip of her tail.

"You haven't seen the last of me, you

Worthless Wonders!" howled Gorgonzola. Then he threw himself off, plunging deep into the river.

A moment later, the last of the royal boat disappeared, and there was nothing left but a little trail of bubbles.

Chapter 9

FRIENDS FOREVER

Tabby was just about to turn away when a cat's head popped up above the water's surface. A long, silvery tail coiled below.

"A catfish!" cried Captain Edmund. "Well, I never!"

Then another head popped up. *And another . . .*

Along the bank, kitizens gasped and

crowded by the water, trying to catch sight
of the strange creatures.

"I haven't seen one since I was a young
soldier in training," said Captain Edmund
in wonder.

The catfish were all over the river now,
floating in the water. Their colorful fur
glowed in the sunshine, and some carried
bright silver spears.

The last catfish to appear had white fur,
a seaweed gown, and a crown of shells.

"Queen Pearl!" said Leo as she swam to
the bank.

The catfish queen smiled. Then she held
something up. It was gold and dripping
with water.

"The Torch of Peace!" cried Queen Elizapet. "Oh my whiskers."

Tabby knelt down in the grass by the river and took the torch from Queen Pearl. "Thank you!" she whispered. "You're true friends of Mewtopia." Then she rose and carried it to King Pouncalot and Queen Elizapet.

"Your Meowjesties," said Felix, and the royal kittens all bowed.

I hope they don't recognize us, thought Tabby nervously. But King Pouncalot just smiled and took the torch from her paws. "How can we ever thank you, Whiskered Wonders?" he said.

"You've saved our kingdom," added Queen Elizapet. "Again!"

"If you'll allow me?" said Captain Edmund. He struck a match and held it to the end of the torch.

Whoosh!

The Torch of Peace burst into orange flames at once. They were so bright that everyone let out a little gasp of surprise. Then they began to cheer.

"We did it!" whispered Felix happily.

As Tabby looked around, she saw that no one was arguing anymore. In fact, kitizens were hugging one another. Even the guards were shaking paws, and saying they were sorry for hurting one another's feelings.

"Where do you think that stinky old Gorgonzola went?" wondered Leo.

"I see him!" shouted Captain Edmund suddenly. "He's getting away!"

Turning, Tabby saw that Gorgonzola had climbed out of the water and into a little basket boat, just like the ones the three kittens had used to go down the river. He began to paddle with his claws.

"Get him!" cried Queen Elizapet.

Queen Pearl waved a webbed paw. Three catfish swam through the river, chasing after the rat king.

"Do you think they'll catch him?" said Felix as Gorgonzola disappeared around a curve of the river.

But before Tabby could reply, she found

herself lifted up onto the shoulders of a guard, along with Felix and Leo, so the whole crowd could see them.

"Three cheers for the Whiskered Wonders!" called King Pouncalot. "Hip hip . . . hooray!"

Tabby felt her tail curling in embarrassment as the kitizens cheered, along with the catfish. But she still grinned.

When it was over, and the guards had put Tabby and her brothers down, King Pouncalot and Queen Elizapet turned to Queen Pearl.

"We must thank you, too," said Queen Elizapet, "for returning our torch to us."

"We thought we'd never see you again!" added King Pouncalot. "You stopped coming to our Peace Parades."

"You stopped inviting us!" said Queen Pearl.

King Pouncalot and Queen Elizapet shared a puzzled look.

"Oh dear," said Queen Elizapet. "The invitations must have gotten lost in the current!"

"Just like our toy boat!" whispered Leo.

"We *always* want you to come to our parades," said King Pouncalot. "You catfish build the loveliest boats I've ever seen!"

Queen Pearl blinked. "You really mean it?"

"Of course!" said King Pouncalot and Queen Elizapet together.

The catfish queen smiled. "Then we will!"

"Excellent!" Queen Elizapet clapped her paws together. "Let's start this parade all over again! And this time, it will be the best we've ever had. We'll show that land cats and catfish will be friends forever. Come along, everyone! Let's get the boats ready. We'll need a new royal boat, of course . . ."

As the guards and kitizens hurried around, Tabby flicked her ears to signal to her brothers. Together, they slipped away. They ran behind the big tent where they had left their clothes, and pulled them on over their costumes. In no time at all, they were royal kittens once again.

They found Nanny Mittens snoozing in the chair where they'd left her, with her hat over her face. A little pile of empty plates and teacups sat at her elbow. Leo threw his paws around Nanny Mittens's leg in a big hug, and she stirred and sat up.

"Goodness!" she said, ruffling Leo's ears. "I must have dozed off . . . Did I miss much?"

"Not really," said Tabby, trying not to smile.

"Just King Gorgonzola trying to take over Mewtopia again!" said Leo.

"But the Whiskered Wonders stopped

him," added Felix quickly. "Everything's fine now!"

"Oh my whiskers," said Nanny Mittens.

"There you are!" cried King Pouncalot from outside the tent.

The royal kittens turned to see their parents hurrying toward them. The king and queen swept all three of them up in a tight hug.

"Thank goodness you're safe!" said Queen Elizapet. "But what a shame. You missed the Whiskered Wonders again!"

"You do have terrible luck with them," said King Pouncalot. "You should have seen them! They were so brave. They really taught that wicked Gorgonzola a lesson."

"They sound amazing!" said Leo, grinning.

"Maybe we'll see them next time," said Tabby, winking at her brothers.

"Come along," said Queen Elizapet. "The parade is about to begin!"

"And this time, you can come on the boat with us," said King Pouncalot. "We think *you've* learned your lesson, too. I know we have!"

Tabby shared a grin with her brothers. *I can't wait!*

Soon afterward, the Peace Parade was in full swing. Tabby's parents had chosen Suki's little fishing boat to use as the new royal boat. "It's not very fancy," said Queen Elizapet, "but that doesn't matter. It was good enough for the Whiskered Wonders, so it's good enough for us!"

Captain Edmund held the Torch of Peace. It burned brightly, the orange flames leaping up high. Tabby and her brothers leaned over the side next to him, pointing out the best-decorated boats in the parade. They waved to kitizens on the banks and to the catfish, who leaped and swam in the water below, darting in circles around the boats.

"I think the catfish like the boats even more than we do!" said Felix.

"The Peace Parade has really brought

everyone together," sighed Tabby happily. She watched as a group of catfish gave some laughing kittens a ride on their shoulders.

"Take that, Gorgonzola!" said Leo, punching the air. "That rotten rat's no match for Mewtopia!"

I hope you're right, thought Tabby.

She had a funny feeling that they hadn't seen the last of the rat king. But one thing was for sure—he hadn't ruined the Peace Parade. *And whatever he tries next, the Whiskered Wonders will be ready for him!*

Don't miss Princess Tabby's next quest!

#4: Tabby Takes the Crown

The royal kittens climbed up into the tree-house and leaned out of the window, watching kitizens in the streets far below. The Founding Day Festival was in the meadow beside the town, and there were lots of kitizens heading there, all in fancy clothes and costumes.

"Look at that costume!" said Felix. He pointed at three kittens walking one after the other, each wearing one part of a huge, silvery fish outfit.

"They look yummy!" said Leo, licking his lips. "Hey, those ones are dressed as the Whiskered Wonders!"

The royal kittens peered down at some little kitties gathered around a cotton catnip stall. They all wore black, with colorful scarves tied over their faces.

"They look just like we do in our secret outfits," said Tabby. She grinned. No one in all the kingdom knew that she and her brothers really were the Whiskered Wonders.

"Imagine if those kitties knew the real Whiskered Wonders were watching them right now!" said Leo.

Felix nibbled his claws. "I have a bad feeling we'll need those outfits again . . . King Gorgonzola said he'd never stop trying to take over the kingdom!"

"Who cares about that stinky rotter?" said Leo at last.

Then the kittens heard a nasty laugh from somewhere close by.

Peering down from the treehouse, they spotted three funny-looking figures crouched by the palace walls. They were all wearing kitten ears attached to headbands. But they weren't cats. Their faces were too thin. Their paws were too pink. And their tails were too long and scaly . . .

Tabby's heart quickened.

"Rats!" Felix gasped.

"Not just any rats," whispered Tabby. "It's King Gorgonzola's sneaky servants!"

"What terrible costumes!" Leo scoffed. "We spotted them in no time."

"Shh!" said Tabby. "Let's listen . . ."

As the royal kittens fell silent, Brie spoke up. "Just wait," she said. "This is his best plan yet!"

"His Revoltingness is so smart," said Chedd. "I can't wait until he steals it!"

"Steals what?" asked Mozz.

Brie rolled her eyes. "Keep up, cheese-for-brains. King Gorgonzola is going to steal the Crown of Mewtopia, remember? And he's going to do it today!"